The Gift of Love Is the Key to my Heart

Flairs and Glairs
Publication House

"The Gift of Love is the Key to my Heart"

ISBN No: " 978-93-90799-90-9"

1st Edition

Language – English and Hindi

Flairs and Glairs

Publication House

Regd. Under MSME Act.

Disclaimer

This is a work of fiction and solely represent the thoughts of the corresponding authors of the articles. Our editors have tried their best to edit the content of all the authors and check the plagiarism.
All the write-ups in this book are unique and are only published in this book.
In case any plagiarism or error is found, only the author is responsible alone, and not the publisher or the Compilers.

Cover Designing and Book Formatting
Shubham Shah and Ishani Agarwal

Acknowledgement

Behind every work, we need a lot of effort and dedication. We all go through this tough time which helps us to grow in life. We all have our support system in our life. They help us in tough times. They are our friends and family.

There is love in our life but it is different. It's from our Parents, Brother, Sister, Friends and our Life Partner.

I have made this anthology as a way for readers to enjoy the works done by different Co Authors, and also new budding writers could share talent.

Firstly I would like to thank to Mr. Prashant Milishia my Father, Mrs. Paresha Milishia my Mother , Mr. Vinit Milishia my Brother and Mrs. Maithili Milishia my sister in law For supporting me on every step and encouraging me.

I would also like to thank Flairs and Glairs Publication for giving this opportunity, as well as Ms Ishani Agrwal who give me guidance on every step of compilation.

I would like to also thanks to My dear Co Authors without their hard work it's can't possible to make this Anthology.

Thank you.

Co Author

Shubham Shah (Founder Flairs and Glairs)
Ishani Agarwal (Co-Founder Flairs and Glairs)
Zeel Milishia (Compiler)

1) Mumuksha Makwana
2) Padma Srivastava
3) Sahina Ghugha
4) Archana Devi
5) Krishna Motwani
6) Arundhati Shekar
7) Bhavesh Parmar
8) Rajarshi Das
9) Diksha Motwani
10) Ipsita Panigrahi
11) Arya Ojha
12) Anmol Srivastava
13) Jeevitha S
14) Kalamkaar
15) Christy Gnana Deepa J
16) Miral Dhokiya
17) Nikhil Jain
18) Simran Subudhi
19) Aysha Asreen
20) Jayshree Sahoo
21) Keerthna Surya
22) Shashank Srivastava
23) Mohanpriya.K
24) Ms Ishrat Jahan Noormohammed Khan
25) Amritanshu Shreshth
26) Rashmi Baweja
27) Pooja Vishwakarma

28) Nivetha Rc
29) Rama Dubbaka
30) Prakriti Shreshtha
31) Pragyan Panda
32) Yamini Sona Vaishnavi
33) Suryansh Talwar
34) Ritvik Srivastava
35) Bhavika Dhiraj Sindhi
36) Divyanshu Singh
37) Devendra Fagna
38) Adrija Paul
39) Urja Motwani
40) Jyotipuja
41) Jasmine Panda
42) Shaheen Ansari
43) Nilofar Farooqui Tauseef
44) Ankita Bhatia
45) Abhi Rajput
46) Sagar Chauhan
47) Keyur Patadiya
48) Parth Mistry
49) Riya Singh
50) Dhruv

Shubham Shah

(Founder- Flairs and Glairs)

Shubham Shah, an entrepreneur at “Flairs & Glairs” a brand with dynamics in events organizing and cultural educational pan INDIA, is a 26yrs old guy who recently has entered the digital platform of imprinting emotions. He has initiated with his own open mic platform to help budding poets and aspiring writers under his brand named as “Teekhe Zasbaaat”

He is a commerce graduate from the Bhagalpur City of Bihar. He states Writing has impersonated him since childhood and he has now been writing for over a decade!
Cooking, on the other hand, is his passion! He also mentions, trying out new things just tickles him!
When asked sir, Why SPICY EMOTIONS?
He smiled and added, "agar jasbaat teekhe na ho toh wo jasbaat kahan" Spices are all that blends! So do his words!
As a chef, he presents to you his dish! Hot and freshly served! Taste it! Feel it! Enjoy it! You can also find his writing in the Book "Teekhe Zasbaaat" and 50+ Co-authored anthologies. With his passion to explore opportunities across Platforms, he is working with keen devotion and We wish him all the very best for his future ventures.
He is Featured in the **International Magazine De-Mode** for his upcoming solo novel.
He is **Approved by Ne8x for its Lit Fest,** and is a **Golden Star Awards 2020 Winner.**
He is an **India Book of Records Holder** for his Anthology **Satrang,** and has the **Grandmaster** title by **Asia Book of Records**, for the same.
He has also been featured in **Prabhat Khabar**, **Dainik Jagran** and other renowned Newspaper for his achievements. He has also been awarded with **India Star Republic Award 2021.**
He has been a proud co-author to
India Book of Records (Title- Black)
World Book of Records (Title -15 Wonders of Poetries)
India Book of Records (Title - Aaina)
Vajra World Records Holder (Title - Gustakhi Maaf Hai)
High Range of Records Holder (Title - Gustakhi Maaf Hai)

Share your reviews on his

INSTAGRAM

@spicy_emotions
@shubham4shah

Or via email on

shubham2shah@gmail.com

To stay tuned to his work and opportunities follow his business Handles

INSTAGRAM FACEBOOK YOUTUBE

@flairsandglairs
@teekhezasbaaat

WEBSITE:

https://flairsandglairs.in/
https://flairsandglairs.com/

Ishani Agarwal

(Co-Founder- Flairs and Glairs)

Ishani Agarwal hails from the City of Joy, Kolkata.
She is the co-founder of her Community "Teekhe Zasbaaat" and Flairs and Glairs Publication.
Been a Compiler for 45+ Anthologies, she is in the process for more. Co-authored in 150+ Anthologies. She is a India Book of Records Holder, a Vajra World Records Holder, a High Range of Records Holder and a Bravo Record holder.

Approved by Ne8x for its Lit Fest 2020, and Literary Icon 2020. Also a Golden Star Awards Winner 2020.
She has also been awarded with India Star Republic Award 2021.
She has been featured by the National Magazine "Taree Zameen Par" with the title 'unstoppable'.
Also featured in the International Magazine DeMode for her upcoming solo novel, she is proud to write on social issues, and is happy with the love she is receiving.
Connect with her on Instagram: @Ishani_agarwal_quotes / @compilations_so_far

Zeel Milishia
(Compiler)

Zeel Milishia is from Ahmedabad, Gujarat. She is an excellent writer. Currently she is working as a CO author and a compiler. She loves to express her emotion and thoughts via poetry, shayari, stories. Till now she has been a part of 20 anthologies and had contributed to the process of compilation. She is a linguistic person as she speaks Gujarati ,Hindi and English in her shayari, poetry and stories which can be easily understand and be relatable to human .You can find her writing content via her intagram handle @written_by_zeel.

देखा है तुमको जबसे मानो
दिल कहीं गुमसुम खो गया है
जैसे भवरे के लिए एक फूल
फूलो के गुलदस्ते की मेहक

मिलते है हम जब भी मानो
उल्फत बहुत आता है तुमपे
फिरसे मिलने का ख्वाब आता है
मिलती है जन्नत तेरी बाहों मैं

तेरा दूर रहना दिलको अच्छा नहीं लगता
तेरा इंतजार दिल करता रहता है
तेरी यादों के साथ रहना अच्छा नहीं लगता
तेरा हमेशा वाला साथ दिल को सुकून देता है

तुझे हर रोज दुआ मै मांगती हूं,
मेरी आंखोके सामने तेरा रहना,
मुझे जन्नत से कम नहीं लगता ,
मुझे तेरा मुंताजीर नहीं बनना।

Tu chatpata hajmola hai meri life ka
Kabhi hasata hai to kabhi rulata hai
Kabhi gussa karta hai to kabhi manata hai
Jesa bhi hai meri zindagi ka hajmola hai tu

*

Mere Dil ko aur kuch nhi chahiye
Sirf teri maujudagi hi chahiye

*

Usne pucha ki kya chahiye
Maine kaha,
Tumare Siva kuch nahi chahiye

Khvahise to bahot hai meri
uska pura hona tere bina possible nhi
Kyuki meri har khvahis
Tujhse hi sharu tujpe hi khatam

Mumuksha Makwana

Mumuksha Makwana is from Ahmadabad, Gujarat. She is an excellent writer . She loves to express her emotion and thoughts via a poetry , shayari. She is linguistic person as she speaks Gujarati, Hindi and English in her shayari which can be easily understand and be relatable to human.

Meri zyada bade koi sapne nhi hai tumare sath
Bas ek chhoti si khwais hai ki
Taro se bhari raat ho
Aur samne ladakh ho

Sukun kya hai yeh hum nahi jaante !
Shayad yeh wahi hai Jo tumse bat karne se milta hai

Padma Srivastava

Padma Srivastava, a student with a skillful writer has been brought up in varanasi and started writing from her childhood. Varanasi is also her birth place. She is fond of singing and writing and composing poetry. Before it she has been co _author of several anthologies till now. Her first anthology got published in TITLI under the Flairs and glairs publication since July 2020. She is a nature lover who is very far from the world in which she lives. She has a deep capacity of imagination.

है प्रेम कुछ ऐसा**

अन्जान सी रुक्मिणी, बेचैन सी मीरा और
राधा कृष्ण की जान थी
मिल सकी ना राधा-कृष्ण को,
पर मिलने के बाद भी रुक्मिणी क्यूँ परेशान थी

किसने था त्याग किया नही
राधा, रुक्मिणी या मीरा ही सही
ना मिले राधा को,, मीरा की तो बात दूर रही

हर सांस में बसे थे वो जिनके
राधा, मीरा या रुक्मिणी थी
कण कण में जो बसते थे
स्वयं प्रेम भी जिनकी ऋणि थी

एक मामूली से गाय चराने वाले
यूं ही नहीं धर्म स्थापना में
सहस्त्रों छल वार कर बैठे थे
दुनिया को प्रेम सिखाने वाले
स्वयं अपना प्रेम हारे बैठे थे
जिसने चाहा उन्हें तो कहीं
जिसको उन्होंने चाहा
कहीं हुई पूरी तो कभी अधूरी
ऐसी उनकी प्रेम कहानी थी
राधा, मीरा और रुक्मिणी तो क्या
रह ना सकती थी जो एक क्षण भी उनसे दूर स्वयं पद्मा भी तो
उनकी दीवानी थी ।

Sahina Ghugha

Sahina Ghugha is 20 year old b.com student at Saurashtra university Rajkot. She is from Jamnagar city of Gujarat. She is state level winner in poetry competition 2017. She is Co-author of 15+ anthologies. She is an amazing writer and poet and she wants do something for society through her pen.

Insta ID:-
Itz_Sahina_write

तू अधूरी आस, तू ही ज़िन्दगी की प्यास है।
तू जैसे तरसती इन आंखो की अरदास है।
कभी तू खुशियां मेरी, कभी तू ही उदास है।
तू ही लगे धड़कन मेरी, तू "साह" की सांस है।

तू समेट मुझको खुद में, चांदनी बसे चंदा में जैसे।
समझ ना पाऊं नखरे तेरे, सादा हूं बंदा मै जैसे।
तू शीतल जल सी बहेती, मैं किनारा गंदा हूं जैसे।
मैं नरखट किशन जैसा, तू मुझे सुधारे वो डंडा जैसे।

मैं घनघोर सी रात्रि, तू इसमें चमकते तारो सी।
मैं ठहेरा पवन का जोका, तू हवाएं हज़ारों सी।
मैं भटकु दरिया की तलाश में, तू मेरे किनारों सी।
मैं मुर्जा हुआ फूल, तू है अनगिनत बहरो सी।

Archana devi

She just started her career as a co-author.she received good comments from her readers which triggered her to write more. She also tries to write quotes which could match others feelings.

You look like nothing happened
Giving a smile to comfort others
Deep inside your soul is damped
I can see it in your eyes
Cause I know you to the hell
And love you to the core

Krishna Motwani

Krishna Motwani is a Student currently. She use to pen down her feelings. She is a moody girl. She started writing in the month of june,2020. She writes in her free time. She writes some motivational quotes or poetries too and practices artworks also.She lives her life like a bird As bird flies freely and enjoys life like that she also lives her life freely and enjoy fullest.For motivating and inspiring poems and quotes, you can check her on instagram : @ unique__blog_

Open letter to My Mother: My first love!!

My dearest Mom,

You are my love, you are closest to my heart, you are my secret keeper, you are my world!!

I know you have many works at home then too you always take perfect care of me. Whether i got some cold and fever, you don't even sleep at night. You helps me in studies, you tells me stories befor sleep!

You know, whenever you scolds me i feel like odd and it bit hurts me, but i know you scolds me for my mistakes, which i don't do in future again.
You teaches me like a teacher, you loves me like a sister, you keeps my secrets like a friend, you are my best mumma!! If you will not be there for me in my life, then God knows What i would be now!

You always gives me hope that i will reach my goal soon, you teaches me to have patience, you gives strength to face the problems of life, you always emphasis me to move ahead!

You are the one whom i can share each and everything, which i cannot share with others. Without you i am nothing! You always says one line whenever i fails in some work, 'Let it go, just take a new step with a new hope.'

I love you so much Mom!

Never leave me alone!!

Arundhati Shekar

Arundhati Shekar is a student who is pursuing her graduation in commerce and a Company Secretarialship.
She started to write when she was 17 years old and the passion continued, as of now she has written about 250 poems, she mostly writes about self love, love, friendship, confidence. She has an audience of about 800 people on Instagram and most of her poems are related by all of them.

you and me are connected through strings,
the strings which cannot be detached definitely,
so not to worry about the fights we do,
and not to ruin the bond by either of our mistakes;

we held our hands unknowingly,
and never failed to create our own special vibes,
so, let's just walk together,
holding each other's hands,
making moments memorable,
live the life we deserve,
love the life we live;

I was always that person,
who experiences more in the dark;

how would I tell you about the bottled emotions,
words falling down, giving me no notice as such;

she came through the waves,
the waves filled with emotions and love;

her mind seems to be more attractive,
more attractive than that of her beauty;

you were then in my dreams,
and now in my thoughts,
I'm not able to sing something else,
something else but love

;

Bhavesh Parmar

Hello friends, so let tell me what is the secret behind the reality of his name. Everyone knows him by his pen name but no one knows him by his real name accept his closed one. So his pen name is @mummy_s_prince and his real name is Mr Bhavesh Parmar.

He is one of the beth writers and his write up touched everyone's mind and heart because he understands the value of his writing and he also understands another person emotions. By choosing this name he has his thinking which no one can think. By the time people had some special relationship with him and he became very special to them.

Love? What is love? what is called love?
He was still unknown from the meaning of love.
Because he gave up that he does not has the feelings,
When he lost his first love in a crucial accident.

He thought in whom he could be able to find that person,
He thought was it easy for him to fall in love again with a stranger.
He thought why should he need to find someone else like her,
He thought that why he needs to make a new relationship with a stranger.

One day when he was completely unaware of something,
He found someone who has the same thinking for something.
He didn't know what to do and how to react at that time,
He was in the middle of thinking and he finally said yes to her.

Again he falls in love, again he had the same feeling for someone,
But on the same thing, that stranger also has the same feelings.
They both came in relation where they only had love to share,
With the time they understand each other need, respect and care..

.

Rajarshi Das

Rajarshi Das, an 18-year-old boy, who has found his love for English literature recently, and started to write poems at an age of 14, says, that English literature has given him the strength to fight back whenever he was in a pinch. He continues to state that he wills to write, so that his words may comfort many who need something that will help them to move on in life. With his words, he has a goal of making every person who reads his poetry to love themselves and to see the beauty that their surroundings behold. He believes, that to see the beauty in everything one needs a clear heart, hence he wills to cleanse the heart of his readers of all malice, pain, and discomfort thus making them stronger with his words.

Shades of Love

The beauty of love
Is comparable to the flowing river
In a parched summer day,
In every place,
Wherever my eyes go,
I see love in a new way.
The love that all seek,
I fear that none have achieved,
For they are always loved
Yet they fail to see
The unrequited love that they received.
A person can love another,
The same can love nature
And the same person may love storms,
And also love their child
A person can love their relatives
Love has endless forms.
It is a beautiful feeling,
Where the one you love
Is part of your life
For their sake,
You will to live
And also sacrifice.
It has left me mesmerised
The pulchritudinous colours
Of the invincible emotion,
Strong enough to liberate
Strong enough to decimate
If set in motion.
I wonder how love came,
How old of a origin it has
This much to have evolved,
The various shades of love
It colours and enveloped the world,
It is the core around which all revolve.

Ipsita Panigrahi

A carefree, joyful, realistic in practical life but she enjoys to live in an imaginative and fictional world. This is Ipsita Panigrahi, a budding writer, who loves to express her feelings and emotions through writings. She hails from Bhubaneswar - the city of temples, Odisha. She has a passion for literature, as she loves to do all those stuff which makes her happy and literature is one among them. She is likely to be called as a scribbler. She finds peace in gardening and reading books and an artist is also hidden in her.

When you become my book..!!!

When you become my book .
I will always keep you beside me, applying every hook and crook .
You will always stay with me .
You will become my nectar ,from the buzzing bees.

When you become my book .
I will write each and every page of yours .
I will heal your pain with all the means of cures.
I will put down my heart .
I will win every battle which haven't, got a start.

When you become my book.
I will enhance your grace.
I will entangle yours every messed up lace.
I will pen until my heart ceases.
I will protect you from this rabble's teases.

When you become my book.
I will rediscover our old memories .
Everything that tries to stop us,
I will born all the calories.
I will make you free from all the dust .
I will never allow you to fall for lust .

When you become my book.
I will preserve you under my arms.
Whenever you feel alone I will be found there holding your hands.
I will carry you wherever I go .
And you know that together we will grow and glow

Diksha Motwani

Diksha is a passionate girl from Mumbai, Maharashtra. She loves to pen her feelings. She is introvert but her pen makes her extrovert. She is a writer, singer, artist and a poet!

Sleepless me!

Groaning on pillow in nights,
I was missing our hug tights,
Having a tear in my eye,
Was asking myself, you left me why,
Sleepless me though late,
Was searching for your one face.

Arya Ojha

उलझे बालों से है कुछ गहरी रिश्तेदारी,
मैगी नाम से जाने ये दुनिया सारी।
लिखना और बोलना ही है इनका दास्तां,
बनारस जैसे खूबसूरत शहर से है इनका वास्ता।

The gift of love,
It was like a dove.
He was the prince charming,
I was the princess glowing.
It was all like a dream,
A fantasy like a cream.
He was perfect with imperfection,
Important was our affection.
The understanding between us,
Happiness was installed thus.
The charm on her face,
The instilled grace,
The love was the award,
They were together was the reward

.

Anmol shrivastava

I'm "The introvert writer", it's my signature and it defines my nature too

Ek ladki thi.. nam tha uska TARA.. or me uska DHRUV.. aai thi Zindagi me ek rishta lekr..cute sa chehra.. sweet si voice.. or pyaari si singer.. jab wo aai thi zindagi me.. mai usse Durr bhagtaa rehta tha.. usse hurt krta tha.. or wo bechari one sided love me Meri har baat ko chup chap tolerate kr leti thi.. kbhi koi hope nahi thi usee k In return pyar milega mujhse.. lekin fir bhi Meri ek muskaan k lie khud kitne ashqo see nahaa jati thi.. shyd pyar ki taqat hai.. Dhire dhire hum dono bhut ache dost ban gye.. subh ki good morning se lekar rat rat bhar baate krna start ho chuka tha ... dhire dhire uska one sided love both side Wala ho gya pata hi ni chala.. lekin galti Kia tha maine..use accept Ni Kia tha.. socha tha apne birthday par use surprise duga and Sab express kruga.. lekin kehte hai.. Don't regrett when it's too late.. mera plan spoil ho gya.. uski family ne uski shadi fix krdi..then I expressed everything .. I tried my best to express what I feel for her..

"Maano Dil ki baate alfazo SE jayada mere Ashqo ne keh die the.."

Lekin Kya krta.. shadi fix ho gyi.. Maine izhaar Kia.. or use mujhpar deri ka ilzaam lagana pasnd Aaya..
now she is married.. and I realized "THE THINGS LOST ALWAYS VALUED THE MOST".

Haa ab hum baate Ni krte.. hum dono ki raah alag hai.. Jo ek rishta lekar aai thi.. Taaumra ka ek benaam rishtaa bnaa Kar chali gayi..

Haan ab uskaa Nam k aage kisi or ka naam uski pehchaan bnaane laga hai..

Lekin ye duniya aaj bhi humara naam sath hi pukarti hai..
"Dhruv-Tara"

Maana iss kahani ko koi manzil na Mili... But it's not over yet..

One day.. we willl be together.. may be in next birth.. but definitely..

Jeevitha.S

She is a girl with stupendous writing skills. Her heart is a castle abound with unbreakable courage, being contained with enticing dreams. Penning is her way of spreading aesthetic vibes among her readers. Being a literarian is her pride. She loves to be a unicorn amidst the flock of sheep's !

That inconceivable love which i have for him !

To the person on whom i have so much of hidden love . I haven't confessed it to you , and yet i believe that it couldn't have been a best one if i might have confessed it to you . Its a magical feel always. You know something! I include you in my prayers always, and you are always in my priority list . I always crave for your vibes . Seeing you from distance and observing your little actions is such an enticing feel always , i have watched you a million times yet i haven't felt bored even a single time and that's when i realised the depth of love which i had for you . You have no idea how crazily i react while i hear you through telephone by calling you from an random unknown number and hearing you utter an hello in your sweet voice, it always captivates my heart . Stealing your pictures and saving them into my gallery became my favourite habit , my phone's gallery was occupied by your pictures than mine . Let this love which i have for you remain as a secret forever . My mind knows that you are not meant to be mine yet my heart gathers so much of love for you day by day .From someone who loves you secretly , the one who wants her love to be happy with or without her presence in his life

Kalamkaar

This is Kalamkaar. He is from Uttrakhand bought up in Meerut(Up). His hobbies are reading and writing. His interest is in writing. He love writing. He is part of 295 +Anthologies as Co-Author. He won 290 + Certificate in Writing, He Start writing 29 February 2020. He is part of 2 anthology as Co Author going for record and He is omg record holder as Co - Author of Book Called Laposia. He is part of 5 international Anthologies as Co - Author. He is simple and people observer. His insta handle is kalamkaar51 and email is kalamkaar51@gmail.com. He believes in Karma.

प्यार का तोहफा

जब कभी हम मिलते थे, बात खूब किया करते थे
हर जगह शहर मैं घुमते थे।
वक़्त हम बिताते थे
काम ऑफिस का रहता था उस एकदिन ही मुझे मिलने का मौका मिलता था।
मेहेंगा तोहफ़े की जरुरत नहीं थी हमें जो बिताते साथ हम वक़्त वही होता था हमारा प्यार का तोहफा।
बातभी इतवार के दिन हम खूब किया करते थे
उस छूटी के दिनको हम उनके साथ जिया करते थे
तू तड़ाक नहीं आप कहकर हम उनको सम्भोदित किया करते थे।
वो भी हमसे आप से ही सम्भोदित करती थी
हम उनको आप कहते वो हमको आप कहने से रोकती थी
हम उनसे कहते के अपने क्यों हमें आपको आप कहने से रोका।
क्योकि रिश्ते मे मेहेंगी चीज़े नहीं सम्मान देना होता हैं, अपने हमसफऱ को सबसे कीमती प्यार का तोहफा।
हम उनको खोने से नहीं डरते थे, जान अपनी छिड़कते थे
उनसे मिलने के लिए घड़ी की एक एकमिनट को गिनते थे
करले बात अगर किसी और मर्द से किसी जलसे मे मुस्कुराकर तो नहीं जलता था
भरोसा उसकी सच्चाई पार करता था, और किसी को बोलने का नहीं देता था मौका
भरोसा करना अपने हमसफर पर होता हैं, प्यार का सबसे हसीन तोहफा।

Christy Gnana Deepa. J

Christy Gnana Deepa , writer pursuing her Undergraduate in English literature in Madurai, Tamilnadu, India. She is a compiler of two anthologies, SECLUDED HEARTS and THE ARDENT HEARTS. Moreover, she is a co-author of more than 25 Anthologies. A writer by passion and a literarian by profession. You can follow her for more writeups in Instagram as ___budding___writer

SELF LESS LOVE

Loving someone who does not love,
Caring someone who does not care,
Trusting someone who does not trust,
Is Not A Waste of Time..
It is A sign of TRUE and SELFLESS LOVE...

Miral Dhokiya

A - 23 year old passionate writer who belongs to bhanvad, gujarat. Who also has liking photography. Not a professional writer but she became one to express herself. All her quotes are her biography that express her feel of the day.

जिंदगी का सफर उसी दिन से खूबसूरत सा हो गया। जिस दिन इस सफर ने मुझे मेरे हमसफर से मिला दिया।

Nikhil Jain

Nikhil Jain is from Dhule, Maharashtra.
He loves to showcase his emotions through writing, and his hobby is a workaround.
He uses a simple language in his Shayari and poetry, which could be easily understood and which relates to every human.
He started writing due to lockdown.
You can find his writings and connect with him on Instagram @Love.vibes143 or
Email: love.vibes143@outlook.com

हवा बनकर तेरा साथ चाहिए,
दूर हूं तुझसे, तू पास चाहिए,
परेशानियों में घिरे जब कभी,
तेरा मुझ पर विश्वास चाहिए,
हकीकत में मुमकिन नहीं,
मुझे सपनों ने तेरा हाथ चाहिए,
आशियाना संजोया है ख्वाबों में,
उसमें मुझे तू अपने साथ चाहिए,
निहारना चाहता हूं तुझे दिन रात,
इन आंखों में तेरा ख्वाब चाहिए,
ना टूटना ना बिखरना कभी,
इंतेज़ार की एक आस चाहिए,
रस्म ए मोहब्ब्त अदा करेंगे हम,
मेरे प्रेम पर तेरा विश्वास चाहिए,
तेरा साथ तेरा प्यार तेरा दीदार,
मेरे यार मुझे बस तू चाहिए।।

Simran Subudhi

Simran Subudhi, is a passionate writer and has been into writing since her school days. She has always considered writing as her favourite recipe to express one's emotions by personifying every element of life. She considers writing is a reflection of the person we are and every writer is unique in their character and style. She mostly write poems on themes like romance, pain, heartbreak and the dark aspects of human nature. She believes her poems can have different meanings to different readers and is open to criticism. She is twenty two years old and hails from Bhubaneswar, Odisha. She has completed her Bachelors in Computer Science and Engineering. She got opportunities to work in the MNCs, but she decided to give up the offers to focus more on reaching out to people through her words. She has aspirations to work for the people of her state. You can follow her on Instagram @knowsimran and Facebook /simran.smiley.35.

You can mail her to simransubudhi2016@gmail.com.

CAN WE KISS FOREVER?

I remember the day of the gentlest rine,
The sky was pink and all flames alive,
Walking hand in hand keeping promises,
For a lifetime of highs and lows aligned.

I remember the day falling into twilight,
Painting the sky with colours of infinity,
Coz heaven had never seen any limits,
For metaphorically praising dyads akin.

I remember the day past the dusk O' Nine,
With me in thy embrace eternally bind,
And thy tender lips touching mine,
I wished to kiss you for a forever time.

I HAVE LOVED YOU IN THE DARKEST NIGHTS

I have loved you in the darkest nights,
Tip-toed across the thumping flights,
Dared the evitable events of my plight,
To walk in a way as odd as osmium sites.

I have loved you in the darkest nights,
Read my stories of adversities blight,
Thou condemned me of foolish insights,
Yet never recurred the histories of fight.

I have loved you in the darkest nights,
Have crossed bridges of aging lifelines,
From the never ending frontiers ought,
Till the fathomless Blues we shall shine

Aysha Asreen

Aysha Asreen is a beginner who is currently acquiring her undergraduate in English literature. she had published several anthologies and research papers.she had also appeared in national workshops on research writing.

Aesthetic Movement

Love the Common word which we expect from all to give us and to show us.. the word love is common but the relation is not common, love for life ,love for parents, love for friends, love upon yourself . There are some specific and unique love upon a person who has been a stranger and now become an important part of your life, when you thought everything in over and suddenly a light came into your darkness makes everything bright where you trust that angels are still existing, when you thought to keep full stop the person makes you understand and turned it into comma

Where you both give special names for eachother love each other endlessly. Where you come to a place that you have to live with them for rest of ur life that where you give them the love they missed, where you give them the relation they want, where you give them a way to escape for bitter world ,where they find peace in you, where they find themselves in you ,where they find their lost hope and happiness in you, that movement your life become aesthetic the movement when you realize that you both have unconditional love for eachother. Love is a beautiful thing which everyone should experience

Jayashree Sahoo

Jayashree Sahoo is habitant of ODISHA . Her writings started on yourquote,notojo and mirakee like writing platforms. You can search her on yourquote by name of Jaya Jayashree . Nowadays She is member of many writing communities and earned a alots of certificates through her writings .She is Co.author of 220+ anthologies .Also She is Compiler of many anthologies in Hindi ,English and Odia languages . Currently She is working as project head and board member of a reputed publication . According to her,if you dont express your inner feelings towards someone,then just write those on a paper and making yourself happy for without reason Also she has interested in singing ,travelling ,photography also. Among of these extra activities She studying Nursing on govt medical and she has an aim for be a RN nurse and good writer .

Insta id -@mixing_of_emotions
Email.id- jayashreesahoo665@gmail.com

I love someone

I love someone ,
Who is fully unknown to me till yet ,
Cause I dont want to see him in real ,
Cause I love him in my dream always,
Yes there ,I love someone ,
Who will sure wait for me somewhere
Who will sure love me soemwhere in there imaginary world ,
I feel my love in dream of his love ,
I loving living with his loves
His love may be not showing me
By distance
But Yes ,He loves me
I m also loving him much
But still unknown yet ,
Cause I love someone
Who is unreal in my rael world
Still.I wait for him ,
And loving him
Morend more
In my fantasy dream

Keerthana Suriya

She is Ms.KEERTHANA SURIYA a highly aspired, dynamic medical student, social-worker, a passionate writer and classical dancer who is engaging in self and social development, building relationships and exhibiting integrity. She is Co-Author of various other anthologies.

She is Founder of WACHC Foundation - Women And Children Health Care and also holding the position of Women's Health Empowerment Project Head in the trust Women's Renaissance Centre. She strongly believes that "When women and children rise, their communities and countries rise with them".

Follow her on Instagram - @keethusm

GIFT YOUR LOVE

One of the biggest thing you can do
to someone you love and to
someone who loves you is to tell them
how important they are to you
Every single person deserves
to be loved and appreciated
How beautiful it feels to be shown and
told that you are being loved.
The person who loves you also
deserves to experience the wonderful feeling.
The main reason for separation is
unspoken lovable words
EXPRESS YOUR LOVE
and make your bond stronger every day
Yes! Expression of love is the best gift
one can give to have long-lasting bonds

Shashank Shrivastava

Shashank Shrivastava is a writer from Haridwar. A student of B.sc. He loves to express his feelings by penning it down, also he is the co-founder of poetry event Jazbaat Ae Dil and YouTube channel Jazbaat Ae Dil.

मेरी खुशनुमा जिंदगी की खूबसूरत अज़ल है वो

मतले मकते मिसरे से बनी एक पूरी गजल है वो

अपने इत्र से जो मेरे खेतों को महका दे ऐसी सुनहरी फसल है वो

मुझे संवारने खातिर जो खुद को तबाह कर जाए मेरी ऐसी दर्दनाक अजल है वो।

Mohanapriya.K

Co-author Mohanapriya.K is a good writer from Tamilnadu, India. She has completed her Bachelor's degree in Engineering stream. She has been a writer for one year as her passion. She wants to be a best compiler and curator in future. Yet she sincerely hope that this writing journey of her will bring her many successes. She also loves singing.

Your love is the only key to my heart

We are always together and happy only through the understanding that is within us.
Even if we have small fights, they still bring us closer.
It does not divide us.
I think the gift of my life is to always walk with your hands and lean on your shoulder and cry during my difficult moments.
Even if God appeared in front of me and asked what blessing you want I would definitely ask this is "I want to be with you always".
I am happier than you in all your successes - I say this with great pleasure.
Your love is like an addiction to me,
Because I could not be myself for even a second without thinking about you,
You know the reason!
Waiting for you is always a pleasure for me,
I too am as thin as the wind,
My dreams are filled all around me as the air is spread everywhere,
I will float in the air and fly everywhere through my dreams about you,
For you I am waiting with many dreams in me,
You are with me,
I am with you,
Our love with us,
I will see heaven in this world,
And I will enjoy living in it with you,
Forever and ever.
Be with me always for me.
I am not without your love.

Ms. Ishrat Jahan Noormohammed Khan

Ms Ishrat jahan khan is a passionate Teacher and a Writer she loves reading and writing. Loving and caring is her hobby. And keep learning and accept the positive suggestion is her quality.She belongs to North India and stays at Ulhasnagar (Maharashtra). Loves humanity always.

The Gift of Love

Gift of love is very precious
It sometime is very tedious
It gives a smile
With a different style

It is creating belongingness
With a happiness
It always is a challenge
Without a change

It create heartbeat run
It's a emotional fun
Sometimes gives a nervous feeling
Sometimes it's a very cautious feeling.

Gift of love
Becomes gift of life
Which becomes lifeline
Without any Cline

It makes a bond
Which is not abscond
It's actually a care
Every one can't dare

Amritanshu Shreshth

Master Amritanshu Shreshth is a student of Open Minds A Birla School Kankarbagh, Patna, Bihar std. 9 with an excellent academics performance and a distinguished skill in sports. With a magnificent start at the age of 12 he is an avid writer with a keen interest in life lessons and classical literature with some specific hobbies like playing guitar. He loves to express his feelings and life lessons with his write-ups. He had won many medal and certificates in Literature and Debates with his writing and speaking skills and had written many articles and science documentaries with his pen name Yuvraj.

ALTRUISTIC LOVE

Love, a word which really need someone great to justify its true meaning in this selfish world and by great I mean someone whom you love from the deep core of your heart regardless of any factors to set you apart from them. Love has multiple meanings in life depending on the type of interpretations and conceiving skills as it is a path to free us from all the pains and adversities. It cannot be expressed in words as they are no more than a precious material in this universe. The greatest love in this world is of a child and his mother as it directs you to true meaning of love.

Mom, mother, maa, aai, ammi and many more are the not the path to love but are the destination after taking the path of love which can't be measured as being intense but can only be felt. They are the person who not only acted as shades for us in the scorching sunlight but also gave water to our roots to drive our lives to success and achieve it with flying colours. If life is a flower then mother's love is the divine nectar of it which makes the flower's smell even more good and helps in the growth of it and that of our life. If love is as sweet as flower than my mother is that sweet flower. The mother's love is the purest form of love which need not be acquired but earned by trying to give back the same amount of love to her. Her love can't be repaid as being infinitely large but can be tried to make her happy and charming in every moment of her life as she the greatest gift life has given us

.

Rashmi Baweja

रश्मी इस कहानी की लेखिका बिल्कुल अपने नाम के अनुरूप ही सबके जीवन को प्रकाशित करती है। रश्मी हरियाणा के सोनीपत जिले की निवासी है। उन्होंने MCA किया है। उन्होंने अपना लेखन कार्य 2016 में प्रारंभ किया। वे बहुत ही स्पष्ट वादी है।वे फेसबुक पर HEART TOUCHING पेज पर भी लिखती हैं। https://www.facebook.com/rashmibaweja1993/अलग अलग विषयों पर वे बहुत अच्छा लिखती हैं। उनकी रचनाएँ पढ़कर दिल को सुकून मिलता है। दूसरों के मनोभावों को वे बखूबी समझती हैं। अपने अनुभवों व दूसरों को समझने के अपने हुनर के आधार पर ही वे अपनी रचना लेकर आई हैं। उन्हें इसके लिए बहुत बधाई। आशा है कि उनकी ये रचना सभी को बहुत पसंद आएगी और वे भविष्य में भी ऐसे ही लिखती रहेगी।

प्यार तो खुदा का दिया कितना पाक तोहफा है।
जिसके आगे कीमती चीज़ का रंग भी फीका है।

प्यार तो अपने आप मे ही इतना खास है।
जिसके आगे दुनिया की हर चीज़ आम है।

प्यार तो दुनिया की सबसे खूबसूरत भेट है।
जिसके आगे पैसों से खरीदी चीज़ भी फेल है।

दुनिया मे प्यार का वैसे तो कोई मोल नही है।
जिसे मिले उसे किसी चीज़ की जरूरत नही है।

प्यार दुनिया मे हर किसी को नही मिलता है।
जिसे मिले वो कँहा किसी चीज़ के लिए तरसता है।

प्यार में मिले हर दर्द भी फूल जैसे लगते है।
प्यार के बिना तो हर दिन काँटे जैसे कटते है।

प्यार ज़िन्दगी एक एक खूबसूरत तोहफा है।
जिसके बिना ज़िन्दगी के हर रंग फीका है।

Pooja Vishwakarma

She is pooja. She is a student but she is also a writer by heart. She is from damoh m.p

(1)

जिंदगी एक हसीन ख्बाब हैं
जिसमें आपका आना अभी बाकी हैं ।
जिंदगी एक सुरीला नगमा हैं
जिसे आपको सुनना अभी बाकी हैं ।
आओ कभी इस दिल में,
तो बताए कितनी मोहब्बत हैं ।
जिंदगी आपका और मेरा दिल हैं
जिसे साथ धड़कना अभी बाकी हैं ।

(2)

प्रेम एक पूजा है,
प्रेम सा ना कुछ दूजा हैं ।
प्रेम मन का विश्वास हैं,
प्रेम से भरा हर एहसास हैं ।
प्रेम गीत हैं,प्रेम मीत है,
प्रेम संसार का संगीत हैं ।
प्रेम कभी तपती धूप है,
प्रेम कभी सुनहरी छाव हैं ।
प्रेम जीवन का आधार हैं,
प्रेममय मेरा संसार हैं ।

Nivetha R C

Nivetha R C, a young poetess from Coimbatore, Tamil Nadu. She graduated BA English Literature from PSGR Krishnammal College for Women. Currently, she is pursuing MA English in KSG College of Arts and Science, Coimbatore. She started writing poems from the age of 13. She used to write in Tamil and English.

Nivetha likes to personify the things around her and tries to reveal its emotions through her words.

She is interested to deliver the unheard conversations between two non-living things. She likes to write poems with rhyming words. Sometimes she uses to write acrostic poems too.

Dear Little One

"Hey, little one. How is your life?
Did you miss me? Then give me a high five
Can you realize that you have grown?
Can't, you ask me where I was gone?
Do you feel thirsty, have some water
I have one doubt do you have any hater?
How about your neighbours?
Saw any new birds?
Are you really happy with sunlight?
I guess it made you look bright.
What is your opinion about earthworm?
Are they staying so calm?
Are you ready to listen to my stories?
With a moral lesson which it carries...
Hey, have you looked at a mirror?
Can you hear the water flow in the near river?
How lovely your flowers!
But tell me which are your favourite colours?
Do you love to stand-in rain?
I believe it doesn't cause any pain.
Look at the sky there is a rainbow
They have seven colours. Can you see it now?
Is butterfly your new friend?
Try to have this friendship till your end.
Hereafter I will call you as 'Cutie'
Because it is you who made this place beauty
Trust me. You have an important place in my heart
To tell 'I love You' makes my emotion short.
I trust you can listen to my words
Hey, look at those little birds...
I swear I will not leave you again
Because I can't handle that pain"

My secret conversation with my little plant
Without her to lead my life is what I can't...

Rama dubbaka

Myself Rama dubbaka having a great passion to inspire the people with my words.If anyone was intrested to read my quotes means you can see my Instagram @Ramadubbaka

The gift of love for everyone is mother's love.

When we are in our mother's womb we started falling in love because that is the blood flows into our body and it makes us to react so our love started from that moment onwards...so god given us wonderful opportunity to observe mother's love from our childhood onwards.we are the person which can feel her love from our childhood to her last breath.About mother's love we can't express with the words it is beyond more than that which it will not be enough .For me my mother is my teacher my love my best friend and everything .she makes me happy when i was sad.she encourages me when i was disappointed.she cares for me when i was was ill.Everytime she was taken the responsibility of me.only the Person who understands me in all situations and makes me to be strong to reach my goal.Even this total book will not enough to express my love

So only with one line i can tell that "she is my heart" .Always she is a queen and i am a princess.

Mom's love

My mom's love started by singing sweet lullaby
My mom's care started by sitting and watching when i was sleeping in my cradle
My mom's tears started with sweet affection by seeing my bored laugh
My mom's teaching started when i was doing wrong
My mom's happiness started when everyone was praising me
My mom's sadness started when i was started crying
My mom's greatness started by helping everyone with the name of me
My mom's heartbeat started fastly when was fell down.
My mom's love started from my childhood to adulthood
My mom started everything but not ended anything it will be continued forever.
My mom is great because she is my heart.

Prakriti Shreshtha

Miss Prakriti Shreshtha is a student of St. Joseph's Convent High School, Bankipur Patna in std.10 with an exemplary academics. She is an avid reader and has keen interest in Greek classical literature. She started written poems, short stories at the age of 12 with the pen name Tidal Seashell. She loves to convey her emotions through poetry and quotes. She adores the Greek god Apollo who is the Olympian God of sun and light, music and poetry, prophecy and knowledge, order and beauty. As she cherishes all forms of art, some of her hobbies are sketching and singing. She have won numerous prizes for her art works. Despite of all the struggles in life she hopes to pursue her dreams through her constant hard work.

EVERYTHING FOR YOU

The world around me pun,
Cause I've got an addiction.
This happened long ago,
Cause then my mind was like a dough.

This is my love,
But my mind could'nt let go the dove,
Fear prevails in my mind,
Love has made me blind.

Those eyes are one in which I could let go my soul,
A new carpet is added to my role.
I encounter many sleepless night,
My days are filled with light.

Those hands are the one in which I'll give my life,
For you I'll accept any knife.
I wanna contain all your sadness.
Cause addiction is my case.

I wanna keep this forever,
Always I see they in the Erised Mirror.
You are the meaning of my life,
For you I'll embrace any strife.

Pragyan Panda

Pragyan is persuing her B.Tech in "Chemical Engineering" from IGIT, Sarang. She's a short girl from Rourkela, Odisha. With fascination of nature, she's a spiritual person who motivates people. She does weird stuff like interacting with non living ones and pens down her mind. For more of her works, do follow her IG @quote_love_97.

TO THE SPECIAL ONE

I never wished or prayed for you;
But you did fill my everyday with hopes.
Your positive enthusiasm and vibes:
Enlightened my days and nights.

I accepted every fail being dumb and shy,
I realised then I can fly beyond the sky;
You pushed and dragged me towards excellence_
I was addicted to you and lost my independence.

Your words force blood in my veins,
Even now they keep healing my pains.
Despite so much confusions and fears,
I can successfully wipe away my tears.

You made me realise the value of knowledge_
The spirit of learning and conquering at any age.
In this deception world of fakeness;
You taught me deals with patience.

Well you departed the unexpected way;
Leaving behind your charms in my day_
I was a bucket full of stale flowers:
You taught me living and dancing in showers.

Yamini Sona Vaishnavi

Yamini sona vaishnavi is a budding writer who pursues her III UG of English Literature in Madurai , Tamil Nadu . She has a great love for playing with words and passion for reading and writing , especially poetry and quote writing . She is currently co-author for so many anthologies and wishes to write more . She started writing from her school days , where she used to contribute for yearly magazine and continued the same in her college too . She wishes to touch the hearts of the readers through her poetry .

The love coin :

How can this emotion of hearts be so tough ?
It makes you smile on one side and let your eyes accumulate tears !
It makes you the strongest person on earth , and also , makes you the weakest !
It makes you a funny person and on the other side , makes you boredom's origin !
It makes you a wit someday and also makes you a insane on the other side !
It leaves you in a frightened state of forest , but ultimately gives you clarity !
It makes you the most happiest one on blue and also the saddest one too !
It makes your mind a crystal clear one and also a confused maze at most !
It might teach you good lessons as well as worst experiences for life !
This makes you a good teacher as well a worst guide !
Besides , it becomes a messy land , but also to clean it ,
that becomes a perfect helping hand !
While I sit and think deep about our relationship my love ,
We frequently tend to interchange the tom and jerry characters !
Living with you might seem to be a life of a coin , still it's bliss my love !

Suryansh Talwar

Myself Suryansh Talwar, who writes very often about the thought and some harsh realities of life that many of us don't able to express themselves. I work so that I write and you relate ✍

(1)

Someone to whom I love the most are animals. As the relation that you develop with an animal is lifelong and rigid unlike of that what you build up with man.

Those having pets would be able to explain better the relation they hold with these animals. Animals respond back with all their love and affection and would make sure that no harm reaches us. Whether it is birds or animals, pets have a special bonding with their masters.

(2)

Apart from the bonding they also provide great services to their masters. Like for example, cats and dogs are the most common pets found. Cat's help in keeping the house clean by killing rodents and insects and dogs safeguard the house and keep strangers away. The sensitivity to smell for dogs has been the greatest tool used to hunt down any kind of criminal act for humans. Apart from them, even birds form a great company. Parrots are wonderful pets and they talk so much that it is real fun to be with them. They also inform the owner when strangers are around.

Apart from cats and dogs, horses, elephants, donkeys, camels are all tamed and used by man for his useful needs. These animals help man in several ways and have been of help to man for several decades. Animals also rescue men from danger. There have been instincts where dogs have saved small kids or old men from dangerous situations like drowning or when in an accident.

Ritvik Srivastava

Ritvik Srivastava is an engineer by professional, poet by passion and indian by national. Born and grow up in Rajkot, Gujarat. He loves writing, read novels, musics, long drives, nature photo graphy and he makes content video. He is simple natured person who loves to interact with new people, travel to new destination and explore new areas of life. A boy who has eyes full of Dreams and Heart full of Love.

Mohabatt bhi kya cheez hai
Sirf tujhe hi Taras karti hai
Wo Anjaan se jaan banne ka safar
Woh mein se hum banne ka safar
Wo teri fitoor ki dhoon...
Jo aaj bhi bus mere dil mein hai
Bus khami hai toh.....TERI

*

Ashiqui ek aesi aag hai
Jisme Jalna kabool hai
Jisme doobna kabool hai
Jisme bikharna kabool hai
Jisme kholna kabool hai
Ishq ki bhi kya shatania hai
Barbadiyan aur badlav ek saath lekar aati hai
Yahi toh ashiqui hai

Bhavika Dhiraj Sindhi

Bhavika Dhiraj Sindhi a 25 year old .creative writer. She belongs to Turkey an Indian writing from abroad due to her passion in writing..A bcom graduate..She uses her pen as a best friend to speak her feelings

My clandestine moon..!

In my chaotic and messy life had just ended me in a place where I was all lost...
All alone trying each day and nights to deal with all...
Struggling to get a good job trying to make my family happy...
Dying each day to struggle and survive with all...
The stars and the moon light were my only best friends...
Who saw dealing with all this pain..
I saw time changing..
I saw people changing...
I saw everything changing...

Since then my destiny decided to give me some contentment...
It made me meet you...
The one who took all the pieces of my heart held it and made it all heart..
Since then you made me back to believe in love...
A sorted person dealing alll her pain with smile...
From a stranger you became alll mine...
To my worst days you still brought me a smile...
I just wait for each evening for you and the cup of tea made by your hand all full of love that shall take away all my pain..
I just love the way you do all this...
Just like that you touch my eternity it feels...
I just imagine what would I do without you...
You became my therapist to give me inner peace and calm my anxiety...
The one who made me sleep with harmony..
And thy, you changed my life
In this chaotic life I found my peace...
You came as a blessing in my life and
I'm glad that you made my life colourful..
To the one I know is permanent in my life...

The one who made me bloom in the desert...the flower that you made shined..!!
To my clandestine moon...
I love you being in my life .

Divyanshu singh

Divyanshu singh is a writer and poet from the land of great Rajasthan (bharatpur).His writing skills is lit.He writes only for himself and his loved ones...
follow him on Instagram @chaudhary_sahab_0.5

"बड़ी बहना "

काश कुछ ऐसा हो जाये,
एक बार तो वो लौट आये।
माँ से प्यारी थी उसकी गोद,
एक बार तो फिर से सुलाये।।

प्यार किया था जिसने मुझसे,
मेरी पहली साँस से अपनी आखिरी साँस तक।
वो बड़ी बहना एक बार तो गले लगाये,
गर न सोउ तो एक थप्पड़ फिर से लगाये।।

"उसे लगता है मैं उससे प्यार नही करता"

हाँ माना होता हूँ नाराज ,
कभी कभी गुस्सा भी करता हूँ।
क्योंकि उसे खोने से डरता हूँ,
इसलिए मजबूरन ये सब करता हूँ।।

प्यार करता हूँ उससे कोई दगा नहीं,
जब वो रोती है तो मैं भी कभी हस्ता नहीं।
उससे बिछड़ना मुझे मंजूर नहीं,
मगर कम्बखत किस्मत भी तो मेरे साथ नहीं।।

Devendra Fagna

Devendra gurjar is a writer and poet from the land of great Rajasthan (karauli).His writing skills is lit.His love has no story that's why he start writing.....
#D4VE
follow him on Instagram
@dev_fagna1 & @kuch.adhuri_batein

Dost

यार मेरे नमूने साथ में थोड़े कमीने..
चले थे जिसको भुलाने ,साले लगे उसकी याद दिलाने...

आज नही मेरे कदमों की आहट पहचान लेते हैं,
बिन कहे मेरी हर एक बात जान लेते है..
वो दोस्त नही बल्कि भाई जैसे हैं मेरे,
मेरी आँखों से गिरा हर एक आंसू पहचान लेते हैं..

किश्मत ने पटका दोस्तों ने उठाया..
छोड़ से उस लड़की का चक्कर,
बार बार मुझे यही समझाया

Crush

कोई खता हुई हमसे तो बता दीजिए,
यूँ ना मुह मोड़कर हमें सजा दीजिये..

आज जब कलम से उसकी दो बात करने बैठा,
तो कलम भी शर्मा गयी..
बोली , क्या हमसे इकरार करने बैठा.

इश्क किया है कोई सौदा नही,
इतनी जल्दी कैसे भुला देंगे....

एक बार सही से डूबने तो दे तेरे इश्क में,
क्या पता कभी किश्मत मौका दे या ना

Adrija Paul

"Little hadn't she ever presumed that it'll be this important to her "

Adrija Paul is from West Bengal... She is a content writer on love , friendship and life genre since she was 13. She had been in the marketing team of Bestselling Author Arpit Vageria, she is also a published co-author with a publication house and she loves to pen her thoughts down rather than expressing her feelings to anyone - "Ambivert" , and a Selenophile too.... She had been a part of 10+ anthologies....She is basically a person who started writing about her teen unrequited love."If only he understood life wouldn't have taken such a magical turn like this"Currently she is pursuing her 12th as a commerce student..You can take a glimpse of her @_.adrija.__ and @talesbyunicorn

Falling

I'm falling...
I'm falling for those quarrels...
I'm falling for those liplocked kisses...
I'm falling for those overnight talks....
I'm falling for the small stuffs you do....
I'm falling for your concern ....
I'm falling for the words that came out of your lips....
I'm falling for your care .....
I'm falling for those long rides and , those outings ....
I'm falling for those way outs we made to hid our mischiefs...
I'm falling for your cute smile ...
I'm falling for your brown horizon like eyes...
More importantly,
It seems that i fell for you...
Not with happy endings but with the happy pauses we had....

The Perfect Match Exists

She was an extrovert
While he was a lil introvert .

She liked going with the flow, whatever the situation is like ,
But he was a bit calculative.

She was never concerned about the consequences, while he had already planned the future before doing a single work ...

She was a big time egoist and a moody one while he was the one to calm her down each time and always dealt with her freaking ego ....

They weren't a couple , they were "best friends"

Urja Motwani

Urja Motwani a 21 year old writer she has completed her bmm recently. She is fashion and travel enthusiast and loves to write her feelings

No sugar coated love

If you know me than you know i am not one of those girls who will ignore you reply to your msg late purposely to get more attention from you This generation's idea of love is not my cup of tea what is this ignore for more attention and show attitude

I speak with words my darling i speak with eyes the love, the smile the small gestures is what i need ,don't take me for lavish dinners

because I am happy with a bowl of maggi with you but with a smile and holding your hands

I don't dream of perfect instagram stories but the stories that i can store in my heart

I would appreciate honesty love care & respect

I would happily pay the bill my love when we go out i want equality and love

the understanding of each others dreams

Where i know the story of each of your scars your childhood memories i just don't want to know your today i want to know you past your future plans i want to be to truly known i just don't want to touch you i wanna be able to understand your each excitement and to be able to hear your heart beat when we are near i wanna know the slow feeling of first touch first hand holding the thoughts when you hold my hand I just don't want the title of being us i want a partnership i want US not just you and me just for the namesake type where you are busy i am busy in my world we meet we just are physically there have small talk where we have to think before saying something to each other for me love is more than just being physical and small talks

I am very old school when it comes to love and i am proud where the world pretend in the name of love i have the guts to be real some may think i am not cool cool and stuff but j am happy to be that girl because to love me ,you have to be able to be you and talk and give your time to me & the only thing to get space in my heart is spoiling me not with gifts but with love and care and taking efforts is what i

Jyoti puja Biswas

Passionate dancer and writer

Saath

Love is emotion. A mixture of emotions, beahviours and beliefs associated with strong feelings of affection, protectiveness, warmth and respect for another person.

Every person in this universe fall in love. We all fall in love by chance but we stay in with choice . But mine story is different. I'm not in any relationship but I want to be in.

It's not like that, I haven't got any proposal. I have got many proposal but I didn't accept it. Because I love someone else, I love him from depth of my heart. His nature, his beahviour and no doubt his cuteness, made me fall in love.
My story is complicated. I love him but he don't. Though, he's not in any other relationship but still do not want to be together. No issues, everyone has different feeling for different people. I'm just his casual friend and I am happy. He's with me and that's enough. Tag doesn't matter.

I am lucky enough to have him as a friend.

We met in coaching as mate. I fall in love at first sight. I was not having his number I smartly took it from teacher's Mobile and texted him we both started with "hi" and it kept on going but after one month I came to know he's in relationship. It was really shocking and heartbreaking news for me. I decided to vanish away from his life. It was not easy for me, I cried for months and years. Everyday it was a blunder for me. 2 years passed like that but I was not able to control my feelings and emotions. Then, I thought the only thing matter is that "the person you love most is with you. Tag doesn't matter."

I started to be in touch with him. Again, it started with "hi" and conversation kept on. He's not in relationship now. Last year they broke up.

We both are good friends and I don't want to lose him again because of my stupidity.

I am quite happy and sure want to be his beloved but he don't feel anything for me.

I just want to see him happy, nothing else I want.

Jasmine Panda

Miss Jasmine Panda is presently pursuing M.Sc. Chemistry from Berhampur University, Odisha, India. She is a Gold Medalist and University Topper in her B.Sc. She is also continuing an internship CSIR-SRTP in IICT Hyderabad. She holds the post of Senate Member of the University for the session 2019-20 in Academic Pursuits. She is a Governor Awardee for YRC. She has received All-Rounder Award in her 12th standard for excellence in extracurricular activities along with studies. She has been Literary and Cultural Champion in her college days. Apart from being a versatile orator and debator, she has been a part of 230+ anthologies till now and loves to pen down her feelings! She is an amiable person interested in both Science and Literature, having a wide variety of interests like painting, sketching, acting, anchoring, debating, rangoli making, taking part in extempore, elocution and many more...

कुछ रंग खुशियों के

दुनिया के इस भागंभाग में,
इस भागदौड़ भरी जिंदगी में,
काम में उलझे हुए दिन में,
मीठे सपनों में बंधे हुए रात में,
तुम भूलते नहीं हो...मेरे लिए...
कुछ रंग खुशियों के...
तुम्हारा मुझसे यूं मिलना,
मेरे जुल्फ़ों को सहलाना,
मुझसे बेइंतहां प्यार करना,
आसमान से चांद ले आना!
सच में, तुम भूलते नहीं हो...मेरे लिए...
कुछ रंग खुशियों के...
मुझे खुश करने के लिए,
मेरा प्यार पाने के लिए,
ख्वाहिशें पूरी करने के लिए,
किसी भी हद तक जाना!
सच में, तुम भूलते नहीं हो...मेरे लिए...
कुछ रंग खुशियों के...
महसूस हो रहा जन्नत का,
अनुभव यहां मुझे स्वर्ग का,
बस साथ ही तो चाहिए तुम्हारा,
है प्रभु! अटूट रहे ये बंधन हमारा!
सच में, तुम भूलते नहीं हो...मेरे लिए...
कुछ रंग खुशियों के...
प्यार हमारा, दुनिया हमारी,
श्रृंगार मेरा, तारीफ़ तुम्हारी,
रंग हमारा, खुशियां भी हमारी!
रंग हमारा, खुशियां भी हमारी!

सच में, तुम भूलते नहीं हो...मेरे लिए...
कुछ रंग खुशियों के...
कुछ रंग खुशियों के...
कुछ रंग खुशियों के...

Shaheen Ansari

She is pursuing Masters in Microbiology. And the one who try to put her thoughts in words of her imaginary world with her unique viewpoint. She is a free soul of an utopia with a perspective of protopia. Her viewpoint to see the world have always been come up as the hog heaven were everything is just perfect and fulfilled. To connect with her through
e-mail shahiin.ansarii@gmail.com and also
Instagram - shahin_ansari_22.

Connection with God

Joy, sorrow, pain or love
All will be in journey of life

No matter what happen in life,
But I trust God he will forsake and save me.

When I feel confused or lost
I always turn to God and pray.

I know I can trust him solely,
So better to believe on him rather than people

Also in times of doubt and fear,
I always mumble his name which makes me feel safe.

God keeps me away from going astray
and I will always follow his path.

Nilofar Farooqui Tauseef

Meet our co-author Nilofar Farooqui Tauseef, born and brought up from Bihar Sharif, Nalanda but living in Mumbai. She is Software Engineer in IT and loves penning down her thoughts, emotions through her writing. For her "Pen is a sword to bring revolution". She wants to make a new changes in life by the motivational quotes or speeches. You can check her fb and instagram handled - @writernilofar

राह-ए-इश्क़

राह-ए-इश्क़ मेरा गुल-ए-गुलज़ार हो जाए।
ख़ारों की गलियाँ, सदाबहार हो जाए।

ऐसी हो आहट, तेरे क़दमों की,
पलकें उठे तो दीदार हो जाए।

बज़्म में, तू जो , पास बैठे मेरे हमनवा
ख़ामोश लब हों, आँखों से इज़हार हो जाए।

सरगोशियाँ मुहब्ब्त की, फ़साने रचने लगी है
क़ैद में मैं रहूँ, तू तलबगार हो जाए।

अर्श भी उतर आए फ़र्श पे, क़बूलियत को,
क़बूल मैं करूँ, फ़िर तेरा इज़हार हो जाए।

इश्क़ ही इश्क़

एहसास-ए-मुहब्बत, मुझे संदल कर दे।
शिद्दत-ए-मुहब्बत, मुझे पागल कर दे।
जुनून-ए-मुहब्बत, रायगाँ न जाये,
तपिश-ए-मुहब्बत, मुझे बादल कर दे।
मीरा बन मैं नाचूँ, धुन पे,
बिन घुँघरू मुझे, पायल कर दे।

रूह रहे, वबस्ता उस रूह से,
खंजर-ए-मुहब्बत, मुझे घायल कर दे।
नज़रें करम, इनायत रहे,
उन आँखों का, मुझे काजल कर दे।
महफ़ूज़ रहे, इश्क़ मेरा साये में,
उम्मीद-ए-मुहब्बत, मुझे आँचल कर दे।

ख्यालों में हो, रूह का मिलन,
इबादत-ए-इश्क़, मुझे मुकम्मल कर दे।

Ankita Bhatia

Ankita Bhatia, 20 year old girl hailing from New Delhi persuing BSC second year... An author and entrepreneur..A girl facilitated with 3 awards in last two months named as "Young Entrepreneur of Year 2020" , "Be the Change" and "Real Superhero of Year in field of author and entrepreneurship...Compiler and Co Author of 10+ anthologies...read her thoughts @_purposeoflife_by_ankita on Instagram.

Open Letter to Someone whom I love, My parents..

.

The precious gift is love and thank you mom dad for introducing me to this gift ..The day I came in this world you were the first one whom i fall for...someone whom I can trust blindly not only I but every child.. and dad you ! You are every daughter's first love the only man who will never ditch her daughter who will never leave her no matter what ..and am the luckiest to have you in my life...Words are less to explain the unconditional love that ties a relation between a child and parents

.

Abhi Rajput

Abhi Rajput is an engineer by professional, and indian by national. Born in Surat and grow up in Ahmedabad,Gujarat. He loves to listen musics and long drives. He is simple natured person who loves to interact with new people, travel to new destination and explore new areas of life.

तू मेरे पास है,
में तेरे साथ हूं ।
जैसे एक झील में चांदनी,
जैसे अमृत्व का प्रतिबिंब।
जैसे अमृत्व की झील में चांदनी की रोशनी,
चांदनी की रोशनी में अमृत्व का प्रतिबिंब।

*

कोई कहता है कि शराब में नसा है,
कोई कहता है चिलम में नसा है।
उन्हे क्या पता था कि उसकी सागर जैसी आंखो में डूबने जैसा ओर नसा कहा है ।

Sagar Chauhan

Sagar Chauhan is civil engineer. He has passion to read novel and history. He is born in Ahmedabad, Gujarat. He loves to write about new place and traveling new places, nature photography and fitness. He is simple man with good heart. He love to make new friends from new place to understand their culture and their destination.

Ek baat rah gyi dil me
Jo kabhi baata nai paya
The kuch jaazbaaat jo kabhi bayan na kar paya
Pata nahi kya hua iss kuch halat me
Na tum samaj payi na me tumhe samaja paya

Isaq ki iss mehphil me
Pata nai mohabaat kaha kho gayi
Khawab me dekhe kuch sapne adhure lagne se lage
Par jab se tumhe dekha hai
Lagta ki sapno ko ek aasman mil gaya

Keyur patadiya

Keyur patadiya is an grader by professional, spiritual by passion and indian by national.Born in Ahmedabad and Brought up in Mumbai. he loves to Book Read, music and meditation. He is Simple nature who has love to interact with new people.

Hum aapse dur he koi gum nahi

Dur rahkar bhi tumhe bhulne wale hum nahi

Roz hoti rahe cod or vedio call pe bate

Teri ye sab bate kisi mulakato se kam nahi

Kuch bolu to tera naam yad aata he
Kuch sochu to tera khayal aata he
Kab tak chupau dil ki bat ko
Muje to har jagah tuhi najar ati he

Parth Mistry

Parth Mistry is a Computer engineering student , poet by passion and indian by nation. Born and grow up in Ahmedabad, Gujarat. He loves music ,He plays Guitar , piano and also choreographs dance . He is simple natured person who loves to follow his passion, travel to new destination and enjoy his surroundings. A person with heart warming nature.

Pyaar me dil tutne k baad dar b dar bhatke reh jaoge
Pyaar me dil tutne k baad dar b dar bhatke reh jaoge
Pr tum use kabhi smja nhi paoge

Uski yaad me aansuo ka samandar bahaoge
Smjayenge dost phir bhi tum khudko takleef dete jaoge
Pr ye sach h yrr tum use kabhi smja nhi paoge

Uske jaaneke baad khana khaana bhul jaoge
Har do do minute apna phone check krte reh jaoge
Uski wapas aane ki juthi umeed dil ko dilaoge
Pr ye sach h yrr tum use kabhi smja nhi paoge

Uski har khushi ke liye apni khushi daav pe lagaoge
Uske aankho me aansu aaye uske pehle uski muskaan lotaoge
Wo zindagi me khush rhe wo dua aur mannate manaoge
Pr ye sach hai yaar tum use kabhi smja nhi paoge

Raat raat bhar uski tasveer seene se lagaoge
Na chahte huve bhi uska hi zikr zubaan se batlaoge
Pehli Mohabbat ke kisse har kisiko sunoge
Pr ye sach hai yaar tum use kabhi smja nhi paoge
Tum use kabhi smja nhi paoge

Riya Singh

Riya Singh, a pen name used by the writer. Her hobbies are in a various fields including from reading a lot to dancing a little. A hopeless romantic girl, pursuing graduation. Belongs to the land of wonders Uttar Pradesh, India. She's quite passionate about writing.

Mine

I woke feeling something wrapped around my waist. I sighed trying to adjust the weight but it doesn't even move. Finally I opened my eyes and notice it was his hand wrapped around me. I smiled thinking about him.

We met each other in college and became the biggest enemy of each other. Every chance we get we start fighting each other. But suddenly the things started changing, I don't know how and when. I start noticing him in different way, something about him starts luring me towards him. He didn't felt same for me, so I did what the actresses do in movies, I left. Not literally I got job offer so I left and this idiot thought I went because of his rejection.

And finally we met in college reunion. He was the same arrogant boy but I had became a little mature. The tables were turned this time. He fell for me and I, well I was single because of the workload.

Suddenly after two days, I received a bouquet in my office and the proposal of our first date. I smiled looking at the offer and politely declined it, saying I was busy with work. But in reality I was squealing, still he rejected me first. The truth was there was always a special place for him in my heart no matter what I did, so at last I accepted. Because I can't force myself to stop feeling for someone and started spending my days in office working for hours.

At last, on his 50th bouquet I agreed for the date. He started opening up to me and I to him. Things were not always good for us just like any other relationship but what really mattered was instead of fighting with each other we tried to sort it out. We did have a rocky start but at last there was a happy ending

"Good morning, wifey." He whispered in my ear and I shuddered from his hot breath. I turned my head to look towards his face and gave him a big smile.

"Good morning, husband." I said looking into his eyes.

"It feels good that you're finally mine." He said wrapping his hands around me. I smiled, before hugging him.
No matter what happen in future, but I'll never regret loving this possessive man of mine

DHRUV

Hola AmigosAn emotional writer of his emotions and and a college student DHRUV this side Born in Indore raised in Gwalior A lion of his parents Shiv Prasad Jha and Rupam Jha

He completed his schooling with CBSE from Gwalior Currently He is pursuing B.Sc(pcm)from Bhopal

Apart from that he is an enthusiastic writer and an athlete He is passionate about his writing and He is hoping to publish his own book someday

He would like to thank his friends who always kept pushing him to give his

best And his everything Radha thank you for always motivating me and coming you in my life is a boon for me

Insta I'd: _the_love_and_pain

Thank you and Love you forever and ever and ever Ayushi

दिलो मीटर वाला प्यार

कि कुछ इस कदर हम दोनों खुद पर संयम रखेंगे
की हम दोनों इन दूरियों मै भी अपने प्यार को कायम रखेंगे
जो लोग कहते है कि दूरियों से रिश्ते की मिठास खत्म हो जाती है
हम उन लोगो के सामने अपने प्यार को साबित करेंगे
कि औरो की तरह हम सिर्फ सोशल मीडिया पर hashtag और
लाइक्स बटोरने के लिए प्यार नहीं करेंगे
हम औरो की तरह पास तो नहीं पर हा हम इन दूरियों मै
अपनी अनोखी यादें सजोएंगे
हा हम एक दूसरे कि गलती से खफा भी होंगे
तो मिलकर हम एक दूसरे से रज़ा भी करेंगे
हम ओरो की तरह अपने रिश्ते पर कभी
 गलतफहमी की आंच नहीं नहीं आने देंगे
और जो कभी आ भी गई ये आंच तो हम इस
आंच की गर्मी को अपने भरोसे की ठंडी हवा से
खत्म कर लेंगे
मै रोज़ तुम्हे औरों को तरह अपनी गोद में तो नहीं
सुला पाऊंगा
पर हा रोज़ रात को मै ही फोन पर बात
कर के तुम्हे प्यार से सुलाऊंगा
हमारे रिश्ते मै सब कुछ दूसरो की तरह ही होगा
हा बस कुछ किलोमीटर का फर्क रहेगा
लेकिन हमारे दिलो के दर्मिया कोई दूरी
नहीं रहेगी
हमारे दिलो कि धड़कन यूंही एक दूसरे मै
पाई जाएगी
हम कुछ इस तरह अपने रिश्ते को संभाल कर
रखेंगे
हम कुछ इस तरह इन दूरियों मै भी अपने
प्यार को कायम रखेंगे

Flairs and Glairs, a platform by a student for the students. We are esteemed youth struggling to carve out our path for our future and we follow a basic mindset Since everyone is not born with all-round skills. Joining hands with people who are born to execute it with perfection is the best way to evolve. Self-Evolution is the need of the hour but, evolving as a community is what we strive for. The initiative as kickstarted by, Founder- Mr. Shubham Shah with the motive to utilize the skillset and talent of writing has now a team of 10+ people who are actively participating into newer forms of learning and discovering talents among youngsters. We Provide platform and services like Publishing opportunities, Open mics, Workshops, Hands-on training. Operating with Brand Name of Flairs and Glairs (Publication House), we offer the chance of elevating a passionate writer to an esteemed author With Brand name Teekhe Zasbaaat. We bring to you an opportunity to get accustomed with the Public Speaking and Presenting of Thoughts along with regular challenges to brush up your inking spirit. The newest initiative to extend our services we introduced in a new writing Platform- The Glittering Fables and Ink Over Tears.

We Choose to Fly Like A Falcon than to be

a Leg Pulling Crab.

To Know More: Infoline – 7781900870
Mail Us At-
flairsandglairs@gmail.com / info@flairsandglairs.in
Or Visit is at
www.flairsandglairs.com / www.flairsandglairs.in
Social Handles- @flairsandglairs @teekhezasbaaat

www.ingramcontent.com/pod-product-compliance
Ingram Content Group UK Ltd.
Pitfield, Milton Keynes, MK11 3LW, UK
UKHW022005190726
13853UKWH00004B/1752

9 789390 799909